POKéMON

JOHTO HANDBOOK

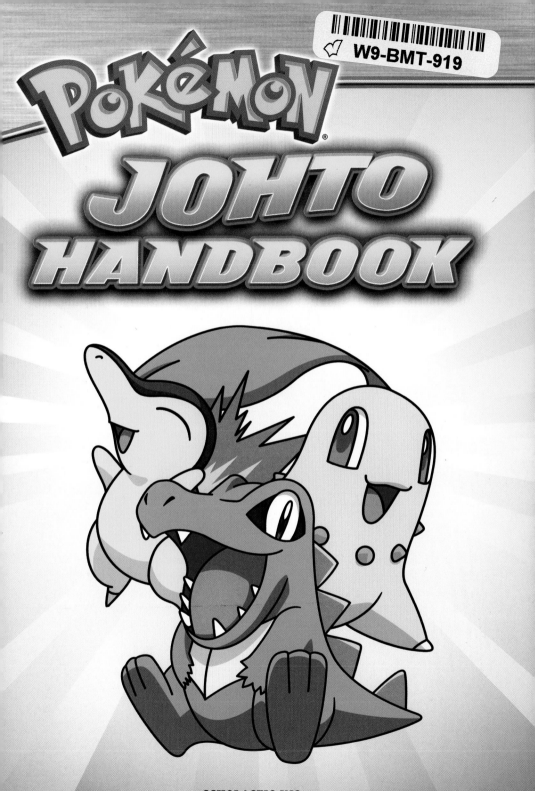

SCHOLASTIC INC.

New York   Toronto   London   Auckland
Sydney   Mexico City   New Delhi   Hong Kong

ISBN 978-0-545-15132-0

12 11 10 9 8 7 6 5 4 3 2   10 11 12 13 14 15/0

Cover Designed by Henry Ng
Interior Designed by Kay Petronio
Printed in the U.S.A.   40
First printing, June 2010

MEET THE POKÉMON OF JOHTO!

In the pages of this book, you'll get in-depth info about over one hundred Pokémon from Johto. We've got everything you'll need to know about 'em, starting with the details every new Trainer needs when choosing between three Pokémon: Chikorita, Cyndaquil, and Totodile.

We've listed all the Johto Pokémon alphabetically, so it's easy to find every one you're looking for. Each entry is packed with useful facts about that Pokémon. Just turn the page for a quick guide to the stats you'll find. . . .

HOW TO USE THIS BOOK

We're going back to basics to bring you the info you'll need.
Here's what you'll find on each page. . . .

Name

Species of Pokémon

How to Say It

Some of those Pokémon names are pretty tough to pronounce!
So we're breaking it down syllable by syllable.

Possible Moves

Each Pokémon has a special set of moves it can use in battle.
We'll show you the moves that a Pokémon can learn as it gains
more experience.

Type

Every Pokémon is associated with a type. (More on this on the
next page!) Some Pokémon have two types — these are called
dual-type Pokémon.

Ability

A Pokémon's special Ability can help it in battle.
Each Pokémon has one Ability. If you see two
Abilities listed for a Pokémon species, the
Pokémon can have either one of the two.

Want to
understand
more about
Pokémon
types? Keep
reading!

Height/Weight

Description

Every good Trainer wants to learn as much as he or she can
about Pokémon. We'll share a few secrets about each and
every Pokémon in this book.

Evolution

If your Pokémon has an evolved form or a pre-evolved form,
we'll show you its place in the chain.

POKÉMON TYPES

Every Pokémon has a type — like Grass, Water, or Fire. Type can tell you a lot about a Pokémon, including what moves it's likely to use in battle and where it likes to live. For example, many Fire-type Pokémon enjoy hot, dry places like volcanoes. They may use attacks such as Flamethrower or Fire Spin. Some Grass-type Pokémon prefer to get tons of sunlight. They may use attacks like Vine Whip and Razor Leaf.

Type also helps you figure out which kind of Pokémon will do well in a battle against another type. Water dampens Fire, and Fire scorches Grass. Flying-types have an advantage over Ground-types. But Ground-types take the charge out of Electric-types.

BUG

There are **17** different **Pokémon types:**

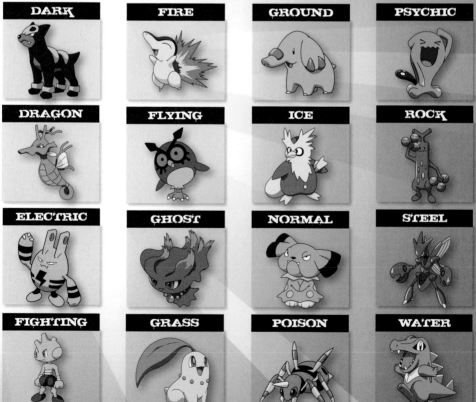

DARK FIRE GROUND PSYCHIC
DRAGON FLYING ICE ROCK
ELECTRIC GHOST NORMAL STEEL
FIGHTING GRASS POISON WATER

OKAY, TRAINERS, ARE YOU READY? THEN LET'S BEGIN!

AIPOM
Long Tail Pokémon

This Pokémon lives at the tops of very tall trees. When leaping from branch to branch, it uses its amazing tail for balance. Since its tail is more effective than its hands, Aipom also uses it to grab things that are out of reach.

HOW TO SAY IT: AY-pom
TYPE: Normal
ABILITY: Run Away/Pickup
HEIGHT: 2' 07"
WEIGHT: 25.4 lbs.
POSSIBLE MOVES: Scratch, Tail Whip, Sand-Attack, Astonish, Baton Pass, Tickle, Fury Swipes, Swift, Screech, Agility, Double Hit, Fling, Nasty Plot, Last Resort

Aipom　　　　Ambipom

EVOLUTION

AMPHAROS
Light Pokémon

Since ancient times, Ampharos has been treasured as a beacon of light for those who are lost. The tip of its tail shines so brightly, it can be seen for miles around. In fact, people once used Ampharos's light to send signals.

HOW TO SAY IT: AM-fah-ross
TYPE: Electric
ABILITY: Static
HEIGHT: 4' 07"
WEIGHT: 135.6 lbs.
POSSIBLE MOVES: Fire Punch, Tackle, Growl, ThunderShock, Thunder Wave, Cotton Spore, Charge, ThunderPunch, Discharge, Signal Beam, Light Screen, Power Gem, Thunder

Mareep ····▶ Flaaffy ····▶ Ampharos   EVOLUTION

ARIADOS

Long Leg Pokémon

Ariados endlessly spins a single strand of web from its backside. It can attach this silken thread to a target, and then follow the thread to its lair. There, Ariados attacks its prey and any companions who happen to be hanging around.

HOW TO SAY IT: AIR-ree-uh-dose

TYPE: Bug-Poison

ABILITY: Swarm/Insomnia

HEIGHT: 3' 07"

WEIGHT: 73.9 lbs.

POSSIBLE MOVES: Bug Bite, Poison Sting, String Shot, Scary Face, Constrict, Leech Life, Night Shade, Shadow Sneak, Fury Swipes, Sucker Punch, Spider Web, Agility, Pin Missile, Psychic, Poison Jab

Spinarak   Ariados

EVOLUTION

AZUMARILL

AQUA RABBIT POKÉMON

Azumarill has natural camouflage underwater — the patterns on its body can fool even those standing right next to it. When it listens closely, it can tell when other Pokémon are in any kind of moving water — even wild, fast-moving rivers.

HOW TO SAY IT: ah-ZOO-ma-rill
TYPE: Water
ABILITY: Thick Fat/Huge Power
HEIGHT: 2' 07"
WEIGHT: 62.8 lbs.
POSSIBLE MOVES: Tackle, Defense Curl, Tail Whip, Water Gun, Rollout, BubbleBeam, Aqua Ring, Double-Edge, Rain Dance, Aqua Tail, Hydro Pump

Azurill ....➤ Marill ....➤ Azumarill

EVOLUTION

BAYLEEF

Leaf Pokémon

HOW TO SAY IT: BAY-leaf
TYPE: Grass
ABILITY: Overgrow
HEIGHT: 3' 11"
WEIGHT: 34.8 lbs.
POSSIBLE MOVES: Tackle, Growl, Razor Leaf, PoisonPowder, Synthesis, Reflect, Magical Leaf, Natural Gift, Sweet Scent, Light Screen, Body Slam, Safeguard, Aromatherapy, SolarBeam

When you're around a Bayleef, you might notice a sweet, spicy smell wafting through the air. The leaves around Bayleef's neck are the source of this aroma, which acts as a stimulant to restore health. It can improve people's moods, too. But beware, because the smell also makes you want to fight!

Chixorita   Bayleef   Meganium

EVOLUTION

BELLOSSOM

Flower Pokémon

HOW TO SAY IT: bell-LAHS-um
TYPE: Grass
ABILITY: Chlorophyll
HEIGHT: 1' 04"
WEIGHT: 12.8 lbs.
POSSIBLE MOVES: Leaf Blade, Mega Drain, Sweet Scent, Stun Spore, Sunny Day, Magical Leaf, Leaf Storm

When a season of heavy rainfall ends, Bellossom are drawn out by the warm sunshine. They are plentiful in the tropics, where they occasionally gather and dance together. As the Flower Pokémon dances, its petals rub together, making a pleasant ringing sound.

Oddish   Gloom   Bellossom

EVOLUTION

BLISSEY
Happiness Pokémon

HOW TO SAY IT: BLISS-sey
TYPE: Normal
ABILITY: Natural Cure/
Serene Grace
HEIGHT: 4' 11"
WEIGHT: 103.2 lbs.
POSSIBLE MOVES: Pound,
Growl, Tail Whip, Refresh,
Softboiled, DoubleSlap,
Minimize, Sing, Fling,
Defense Curl, Light Screen,
Egg Bomb, Healing Wish,
Double-Edge

Blissey can sense feelings of sadness. They are known to be very compassionate. If a Blissey sees a sick Pokémon, it will nurse it back to health.

Happiny ····▶ Chansey ····▶ Blissey

EVOLUTION

CELEBI
LEGENDARY POKÉMON
Time Travel Pokémon

HOW TO SAY IT: SEL-ih-bee
TYPE: Psychic-Grass
ABILITY: Natural Cure
HEIGHT: 2' 00"
WEIGHT: 11 lbs.
POSSIBLE MOVES: Leech Seed, Confusion, Recover, Heal Bell, Safeguard, Magical Leaf, AncientPower, Baton Pass, Natural Gift, Heal Block, Future Sight, Healing Wish, Leaf Storm, Perish Song

Celebi has the power to travel through time, but it is said that it will only appear in times of peace. Celebi is sometimes called the guardian of the forest.

DOES NOT EVOLVE

CHIKORITA
Leaf Pokémon

HOW TO SAY IT: CHICK-oh-REE-ta
TYPE: Grass
ABILITY: Overgrow
HEIGHT: 2' 11"
WEIGHT: 14.1 lbs.
POSSIBLE MOVES: Tackle, Growl, Razor Leaf, PoisonPowder, Synthesis, Reflect, Magical Leaf, Natural Gift, Sweet Scent, Light Screen, Body Slam, Safeguard, Aromatherapy, SolarBeam

Chikorita is one of the three Pokémon new Johto Trainers can receive when they begin traveling. Chikorita loves the sun and uses the leaf on its head to determine the temperature and humidity. Chikorita smells sweet, but watch out! The leaf that grows from its head can be used for a powerful Razor Leaf attack.

Chikorita ....▶ Bayleef ....▶ Meganium

EVOLUTION

CHINCHOU

Angler Pokémon

HOW TO SAY IT: CHIN-chow
TYPE: Water-Electric
ABILITY: Volt Absorb/Illuminate
HEIGHT: 1' 08"
WEIGHT: 26.5 lbs.
POSSIBLE MOVES: Bubble, Supersonic, Thunder Wave, Flail, Water Gun, Confuse Ray, Spark, Take Down, BubbleBeam, Signal Beam, Discharge, Aqua Ring, Hydro Pump, Charge

Chinchou lives in the depths of the ocean. It creates energy by shooting positive and negative energy back and forth between the tips of its two antennae. Chinchou communicates by means of these constantly flashing lights. But it's not just a light show — Chinchou can use this power to zap its enemies.

Chinchou ....> Lanturn

EVOLUTION

CLEFFA

Star Shape Pokémon

HOW TO SAY IT: CLEFF-uh
TYPE: Normal
ABILITY: Cute Charm/Magic Guard
HEIGHT: 1' 00"
WEIGHT: 6.6 lbs.
POSSIBLE MOVES: Pound, Charm, Encore, Sing, Sweet Kiss, Copycat, Magical Leaf

Some people believe that Cleffa came here on a meteor. It's true that Cleffa can usually be found when swarms of shooting stars fall. But they are usually gone by sunrise.

Cleffa ....> Clefairy ....> Clefable

EVOLUTION

CORSOLA
Coral Pokémon

HOW TO SAY IT: COR-so-la
TYPE: Water-Rock
ABILITY: Hustle/Natural Cure
HEIGHT: 2' 00"
WEIGHT: 11 lbs.
POSSIBLE MOVES: Tackle, Harden, Bubble, Recover, Refresh, Rock Blast, BubbleBeam, Lucky Chant, AncientPower, Aqua Ring, Spike Cannon, Power Gem, Mirror Coat, Earth Power

In some parts of the world, people live in communities that are built on groups of Corsola! Corsola must live in clean seas (usually in the south), because they can't stand polluted waters. Corsola is constantly growing and shedding. The tip of its head is prized for its beauty.

DOES NOT EVOLVE

CROBAT
Bat Pokémon

HOW TO SAY IT: CROW-bat
TYPE: Poison-Flying
ABILITY: Inner Focus
HEIGHT: 5' 11"
WEIGHT: 165.3 lbs.
POSSIBLE MOVES: Cross Poison, Screech, Leech Life, Supersonic, Astonish, Bite, Wing Attack, Confuse Ray, Air Cutter, Mean Look, Poison Fang, Haze, Air Slash

Crobat's four wings allow it to fly so swiftly and silently that it's almost impossible to detect. Crobat rests during the day, then becomes active when night comes.

Zubat ....► Golbat ....► Crobat

EVOLUTION

CROCONAW

Big Jaw Pokémon

When Croconaw chomps down on an opponent, it won't let go — even if it loses one of its forty-eight teeth! Luckily, it will quickly grow a replacement tooth.

HOW TO SAY IT: CROCK-oh-naw
TYPE: Water
ABILITY: Torrent
HEIGHT: 3' 07"
WEIGHT: 55.1 lbs.
POSSIBLE MOVES: Scratch, Leer, Water Gun, Rage, Bite, Scary Face, Ice Fang, Flail, Crunch, Slash, Screech, Thrash, Aqua Tail, Superpower, Hydro Pump

Totodile ••••▶ Croconaw ••••▶ Feraligatr

EVOLUTION

CYNDAQUIL
Fire Mouse Pokémon

Cyndaquil is one of the first Pokémon new Trainers may receive when they start out in Johto. If you have a Cyndaquil, don't be surprised if it likes to curl up into a little ball. Cyndaquil are timid, so try not to startle them — if you do, flames will shoot out of their backs!

HOW TO SAY IT: SIN-da-kwill
TYPE: Fire
ABILITY: Blaze
HEIGHT: 1' 08"
WEIGHT: 17.4 lbs.
POSSIBLE MOVES: Tackle, Leer, SmokeScreen, Ember, Quick Attack, Flame Wheel, Defense Curl, Swift, Lava Plume, Flamethrower, Rollout, Double-Edge, Eruption

Cyndaquil   Quilava   Typhlosion

EVOLUTION

DELIBIRD
Delivery Pokémon

HOW TO SAY IT: DELL-ee-bird
TYPE: Ice-Flying
ABILITY: Vital Spirit/Hustle
HEIGHT: 2' 11"
WEIGHT: 35.3 lbs.
POSSIBLE MOVES: Present

Delibird likes to make its nest at the side of very high cliffs. Each day, it carries food to its hungry chicks. If people get lost in the mountains, Delibird will share this food, which it carries in its tail.

DOES NOT EVOLVE

DONPHAN
Armor Pokémon

HOW TO SAY IT: DON-fan
TYPE: Ground
ABILITY: Sturdy
HEIGHT: 3' 07"
WEIGHT: 264.6 lbs.
POSSIBLE MOVES: Fire Fang, Thunder Fang, Horn Attack, Growl, Defense Curl, Flail, Rapid Spin, Knock Off, Rollout, Magnitude, Slam, Fury Attack, Assurance, Scary Face, Earthquake, Giga Impact

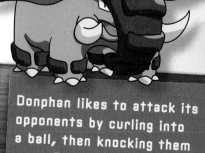

Donphan likes to attack its opponents by curling into a ball, then knocking them over. It can destroy a house with one blow. The longer and the bigger Donphan's tusks, the higher its rank in its herd. These strong tusks take a long time to grow.

Phanpy ..... Donphan

EVOLUTION

19

DUNSPARCE
Land Snake Pokémon

HOW TO SAY IT: DUN-sparce
TYPE: Normal
ABILITY: Serene Grace/Run Away
HEIGHT: 4' 11"
WEIGHT: 30.9 lbs.
POSSIBLE MOVES: Rage, Defense Curl, Yawn, Glare, Rollout, Spite, Pursuit, Screech, Roost, Take Down, AncientPower, Dig, Endeavor, Flail

Dunsparce has wings, but they are only strong enough to allow it to float just above the ground. But if it's under attack, look out! Dunsparce escapes backward by boring its tail into the ground. Dunsparce also uses its tail to dig maze-like nests.

DOES NOT EVOLVE

ELEKID
Electric Pokémon

HOW TO SAY IT: el-EH-kid
TYPE: Electric
ABILITY: Static
HEIGHT: 2' 00"
WEIGHT: 51.8 lbs.
POSSIBLE MOVES: Quick Attack, Leer, ThunderShock, Low Kick, Swift, Shock Wave, Light Screen, ThunderPunch, Discharge, Thunderbolt, Screech, Thunder

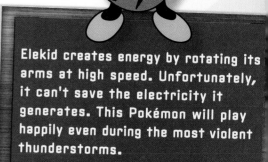

Elekid creates energy by rotating its arms at high speed. Unfortunately, it can't save the electricity it generates. This Pokémon will play happily even during the most violent thunderstorms.

Elekid ···> Electabuzz ···> Electivire

EVOLUTION

ENTEI
LEGENDARY POKÉMON
Volcano Pokémon

When this massive Pokémon roars, a volcano erupts somewhere. Some believe that a new Entei is born every time a new volcano appears.

HOW TO SAY IT: EN-tay
TYPE: Fire
ABILITY: Pressure
HEIGHT: 6' 11"
WEIGHT: 436.5 lbs.
POSSIBLE MOVES: Bite, Leer, Ember, Roar, Fire Spin, Stomp, Flamethrower, Swagger, Fire Fang, Lava Plume, Extrasensory, Fire Blast, Calm Mind, Eruption

DOES NOT EVOLVE

ESPEON
Sun Pokémon

Espeon's fur is soft and smooth — almost like velvet. When it uses psychic powers, the jewel between its eyes lights up. Espeon uses the fine hair that covers its body to predict the weather — and its foe's next move.

HOW TO SAY IT: ESS-pee-on
TYPE: Psychic
ABILITY: Synchronize
HEIGHT: 2' 11"
WEIGHT: 58.4 lbs.
POSSIBLE MOVES: Tail Whip, Tackle, Helping Hand, Sand-Attack, Confusion, Quick Attack, Swift, Psybeam, Future Sight, Last Resort, Psych Up, Psychic, Morning Sun, Power Swap

Eevee → Espeon

EVOLUTION

FERALIGATR

Big Jaw Pokémon

Feraligatr is so massive that it has a hard time supporting its own weight when it's out of water, so it likes to get down on all fours in battle. It usually moves slowly, but in battle, it moves at blinding speed. In addition to its strong Water-type attacks, Feraligatr likes to chomp its opponents between its powerful jaws.

HOW TO SAY IT:
fer-AL-ee-gay-tur
TYPE: Water
ABILITY: Torrent
HEIGHT: 7' 07"
WEIGHT: 195.8 lbs.
POSSIBLE MOVES: Scratch, Leer, Water Gun, Rage, Bite, Scary Face, Ice Fang, Flail, Agility, Crunch, Slash, Screech, Thrash, Aqua Tail, Superpower, Hydro Pump

Totodile ····▶ Croconaw ····▶ Feraligatr

EVOLUTION

FLAAFFY
Wool Pokémon

HOW TO SAY IT: FLAF-fee
TYPE: Electric
ABILITY: Static
HEIGHT: 2' 07"
WEIGHT: 29.3 lbs.
POSSIBLE MOVES: Tackle, Growl, ThunderShock, Thunder Wave, Cotton Spore, Charge, Discharge, Signal Beam, Light Screen, Power Gem, Thunder

Flaaffy's coat can store electricity. Fortunately, its rubbery skin prevents it from shocking itself. When its fleece is fully charged, its tail lights up — and it can shoot electrified hairs from its body.

Mareep ..... Flaaffy ..... Ampharos

EVOLUTION

FORRETRESS
Bagworm Pokémon

HOW TO SAY IT: FOR-it-tress
TYPE: Bug-Steel
ABILITY: Sturdy
HEIGHT: 3' 11"
WEIGHT: 277.3 lbs.
POSSIBLE MOVES: Toxic Spikes, Tackle, Protect, Selfdestruct, Bug Bite, Take Down, Rapid Spin, Bide, Natural Gift, Spikes, Mirror Shot, Payback, Explosion, Iron Defense, Gyro Ball, Double-Edge, Magnet Rise, Zap Cannon

Forretress is almost completely covered in steel. No one knows what lies inside its shell — its eyes are all that's visible. Forretress remain rooted to their trees and scatter pieces of their super-hard shells to drive away enemies.

Pineco ..... Forretress

EVOLUTION

FURRET
Long Body Pokémon

Furret's tail is so long, it's impossible to tell where its body ends and its tail begins! Mother Furret help their young fall asleep by coiling around them. This cute Normal-type might not look very intimidating, but it is quick and a very good hunter. Furret uses its speed to corner its opponents.

HOW TO SAY IT: FUR-ret
TYPE: Normal
ABILITY: Run Away/Keen Eye
HEIGHT: 5' 11"
WEIGHT: 71.6 lbs.
POSSIBLE MOVES: Scratch, Foresight, Defense Curl, Quick Attack, Fury Swipes, Helping Hand, Follow Me, Slam, Rest, Sucker Punch, Amnesia, Baton Pass, Me First, Hyper Voice

Sentret ....▶ Furret

EVOLUTION

GIRAFARIG
Long Neck Pokémon

Girafarig has two brains — one in its head, one in its small tail. This Pokémon is always on guard. It's got its two heads for lookout, and it never sleeps. So beware — Girafarig won't hesitate to bite enemies who try to slink up behind it!

HOW TO SAY IT: jir-RAFF-uh-rig
TYPE: Normal-Psychic
ABILITY: Inner Focus/Early Bird
HEIGHT: 4' 11"
WEIGHT: 91.5 lbs.
POSSIBLE MOVES: Power Swap, Guard Swap, Astonish, Tackle, Growl, Confusion, Odor Sleuth, Stomp, Agility, Psybeam, Baton Pass, Assurance, Double Hit, Psychic, Zen Headbutt, Crunch

DOES NOT EVOLVE

GLIGAR

Flyscorpion Pokémon

HOW TO SAY IT: GLY-gar
TYPE: Ground-Flying
ABILITY: Hyper Cutter/Sand Veil
HEIGHT: 3' 07"
WEIGHT: 142.9 lbs.
POSSIBLE MOVES: Poison Sting, Sand-Attack, Harden, Knock Off, Quick Attack, Fury Cutter, Faint Attack, Screech, Slash, Swords Dance, U-turn, X-Scissor, Guillotine

Gligar likes to hang off the sides of cliffs. If it sees its quarry, it will zoom in and strike. Gligar usually aims for the prey's face, and then clamps down and injects poison. So if you're traveling in the mountains, beware!

Gligar ....▶ **Gliscor**

EVOLUTION

GRANBULL

Fairy Pokémon

HOW TO SAY IT: GRAN-bull
TYPE: Normal
ABILITY: Intimidate/Quick Feet
HEIGHT: 4' 07"
WEIGHT: 107.4 lbs.
POSSIBLE MOVES: Ice Fang, Fire Fang, Thunder Fang, Tackle, Scary Face, Tail Whip, Charm, Bite, Lick, Headbutt, Roar, Rage, Take Down, Payback, Crunch

Despite Granbull's fierce looks, it is actually very timid. But if Granbull gets angry, look out! It will attack with its fangs, and its bite is very powerful.

Snubbull ....▶ **Granbull**

EVOLUTION

27

HERACROSS

Single Horn Pokémon

HOW TO SAY IT:
HAIR-uh-cross
TYPE: Bug-Fighting
ABILITY: Swarm/Guts
HEIGHT: 4' 11"
WEIGHT: 119.0 lbs.
POSSIBLE MOVES: Night Slash, Tackle, Leer, Horn Attack, Endure, Fury Attack, Aerial Ace, Brick Break, Counter, Take Down, Close Combat, Reversal, Feint, Megahorn

Heracross live in forests, where they come together to hunt for honey. They hate to be interrupted while enjoying their favorite snack, and they'll use their huge horns to attack any unwanted guests. Because of the tremendous strength in their legs and claws, Heracross can pick up their foes and throw them great distances.

DOES NOT EVOLVE

HITMONTOP

Handstand Pokémon

HOW TO SAY IT: HIT-mon-TOP
TYPE: Fighting
ABILITY: Intimidate/Technician
HEIGHT: 4' 07"
WEIGHT: 105.8 lbs.
POSSIBLE MOVES: Revenge, Rolling Kick, Focus Energy, Pursuit, Quick Attack, Triple Kick, Rapid Spin, Counter, Feint, Agility, Gyro Ball, Detect, Close Combat, Endeavor

Hitmontop is so comfortable on its head that it fights that way! As it fights, it spins around. The energy it builds while spinning increases its power enormously. Hitmontop has been known to revolve so quickly that it creates a hole in the ground.

Tyrogue ····▶ Hitmontop

EVOLUTION

HO-OH
LEGENDARY POKÉMON
Rainbow Pokémon

Ho-Oh soars through the sky without ever stopping. Its feathers are seven different colors, and rainbows form behind it when it flies through the sky. According to legend, those who spot Ho-Oh will find everlasting happiness.

HOW TO SAY IT: *HOE*-OH
TYPE: Fire-Flying
ABILITY: Pressure
HEIGHT: 12' 06"
WEIGHT: 438.7 lbs.
POSSIBLE MOVES: Whirlwind, Weather Ball, Gust, Brave Bird, Extrasensory, Sunny Day, Fire Blast, Sacred Fire, Punishment, AncientPower, Safeguard, Recover, Future Sight, Natural Gift, Calm Mind, Sky Attack

DOES NOT EVOLVE

HOOTHOOT
Owl Pokémon

HOW TO SAY IT: *HOOT*-HOOT
TYPE: Normal-Flying
ABILITY: Insomnia/Keen Eye
HEIGHT: 2' 04"
WEIGHT: 46.7 lbs.
POSSIBLE MOVES: Tackle, Growl, Foresight, Hypnosis, Peck, Uproar, Reflect, Confusion, Take Down, Air Slash, Zen Headbutt, Extrasensory, Psycho Shift, Roost, Dream Eater

Hoothoot are nocturnal — they only come out at night. These Normal-and-Flying-types stand on one foot at a time, and they change feet so quickly that it's hard to spot. Even when attacked, Hoothoot will stay on one foot. Hoothoot keep track of time very precisely, by moving their heads at regular intervals.

Hoothoot ····▷ Noctowl

EVOLUTION

HOPPIP
Cottonweed Pokémon

HOW TO SAY IT: HOP-pip
TYPE: Grass-Flying
ABILITY: Chlorophyll/
Leaf Guard
HEIGHT: 1' 04"
WEIGHT: 1.1 lbs.
POSSIBLE MOVES: Splash,
Synthesis, Tail Whip,
Tackle, PoisonPowder,
Stun Spore, Sleep Powder,
Bullet Seed, Leech Seed,
Mega Drain, Cotton Spore,
U-turn, Worry Seed, Giga
Drain, Bounce, Memento

Hoppip are so light, they can get blown away in the wind! When they want to stay put, they grip the ground tightly with their tiny feet or huddle together in groups. It sounds unlikely, but these little Pokémon actually do enjoy light breezes. When they are spotted arriving at a destination, it is said that spring is on the way.

Hoppip ·····▶ Skiploom ·····▶ Jumpluff   EVOLUTION

HOUNDOOM
Dark Pokémon

When other Pokémon hear Houndoom's eerie howls, they flee back to their nests. In ages past, it was believed that these howls were actually the grim reaper's cry. The fire Houndoom expels from its mouth is said to be so powerful, the suffering it causes will never cease.

HOW TO SAY IT: HOWN-doom
TYPE: Dark-Fire
ABILITY: Early Bird/ Flash Fire
HEIGHT: 4' 07"
WEIGHT: 77.2 lbs.
POSSIBLE MOVES: Thunder Fang, Leer, Ember, Howl, Smog, Roar, Bite, Odor Sleuth, Beat Up, Fire Fang, Faint Attack, Embargo, Flamethrower, Crunch, Nasty Plot

Houndour ....➤ Houndoom

EVOLUTION

HOUNDOUR
Dark Pokémon

HOW TO SAY IT: HOWN-dowr
TYPE: Dark-Fire
ABILITY: Early Bird/
Flash Fire
HEIGHT: 2' 00"
WEIGHT: 23.8 lbs.
POSSIBLE MOVES: Leer,
Ember, Howl, Smog, Roar,
Bite, Odor Sleuth, Beat Up,
Fire Fang, Faint Attack,
Embargo, Flamethrower,
Crunch, Nasty Plot

Houndour are pack Pokémon. They use different pitches in their cries to communicate with others of their kind. Houndour work together to hunt down prey, and they use their special barks to check one another's locations.

Houndour   Houndoom   EVOLUTION

IGGLYBUFF
Balloon Pokémon

HOW TO SAY IT: IG-lee-buff
TYPE: Normal
ABILITY: Cute Charm
HEIGHT: 1' 00"
WEIGHT: 2.2 lbs.
POSSIBLE MOVES: Sing, Charm, Defense Curl, Pound, Sweet Kiss, Copycat

Igglybuff's body is as springy as a balloon! If it starts to roll, look out! It will bounce all over the place, and you'll have a hard time stopping it.

Igglybuff ····▷ Jigglypuff ····▷ Wigglytuff

EVOLUTION

JUMPLUFF
Cottonweed Pokémon

This little Grass-and-Flying-type floats on the wind. Wherever it lands, it scatters its spores. Jumpluff often end up leaving spores all over the world.

HOW TO SAY IT: JUM-pluff
TYPE: Grass-Flying
ABILITY: Chlorophyll/ Leaf Guard
HEIGHT: 2' 07"
WEIGHT: 6.6 lbs.
POSSIBLE MOVES: Splash, Synthesis, Tail Whip, Tackle, PoisonPowder, Stun Spore, Sleep Powder, Bullet Seed, Leech Seed, Mega Drain, Cotton Spore, U-turn, Worry Seed, Giga Drain, Bounce, Memento

Hoppip ..... ▶ Skiploom ..... ▶ Jumpluff

EVOLUTION

KINGDRA
Dragon Pokémon

HOW TO SAY IT: KING-dra
TYPE: Water-Dragon
ABILITY: Swift Swim/Sniper
HEIGHT: 5' 11"
WEIGHT: 335.1 lbs.
POSSIBLE MOVES: Yawn, Bubble, SmokeScreen, Leer, Water Gun, Focus Energy, BubbleBeam, Agility, Twister, Brine, Hydro Pump, Dragon Dance, Dragon Pulse

Kingdra lives in caves on the floor of the sea, where it hides to build up its energy. According to legend, when it wakes up and yawns, it creates tornadoes and giant whirlpools!

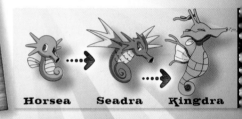

Horsea → **Seadra** → **Kingdra**

LANTURN
Light Pokémon

HOW TO SAY IT: LAN-turn
TYPE: Water-Electric
ABILITY: Volt Absorb/Illuminate
HEIGHT: 3' 11"
WEIGHT: 49.6 lbs.
POSSIBLE MOVES: Bubble, Supersonic, Thunder Wave, Flail, Water Gun, Confuse Ray, Spark, Take Down, Stockpile, Swallow, Spit Up, BubbleBeam, Signal Beam, Discharge, Aqua Ring, Hydro Pump, Charge

Lanturn is nicknamed "The Deep-Sea Star." It creates bright bursts of light, which it uses to blind its prey. Then it gulps the unlucky victim in one bite! It is said that Lanturn's light is so bright it can illuminate the sea's surface from a great depth.

Chinchou → **Lanturn**

EVOLUTION

LARVITAR
Rock Skin Pokémon

HOW TO SAY IT: LAR-vuh-tar
TYPE: Rock-Ground
ABILITY: Guts
HEIGHT: 2' 00"
WEIGHT: 158.7 lbs.
POSSIBLE MOVES: Bite, Leer, Sandstorm, Screech, Rock Slide, Scary Face, Thrash, Dark Pulse, Payback, Crunch, Earthquake, Stone Edge, Hyper Beam

Born deep below the ground, Larvitar must eat its way out! It swallows soil till it reaches the surface. If it eats as much as a mountain, it will snooze as it grows.

Larvitar   Pupitar   Tyranitar

EVOLUTION

LEDIAN
Five Star Pokémon

Ledian gets its energy from the stars. When there are a lot of stars out at night, the patterns on its back change in size. Some nights, when the stars flare in and out, Ledian will flit around sprinkling glowing powder.

HOW TO SAY IT: LEH-dee-an
TYPE: Bug-Flying
ABILITY: Swarm/Early Bird
HEIGHT: 4' 07"
WEIGHT: 78.5 lbs.
POSSIBLE MOVES: Tackle, Supersonic, Comet Punch, Light Screen, Reflect, Safeguard, Mach Punch, Baton Pass, Silver Wind, Agility, Swift, Double-Edge, Bug Buzz

Ledyba ••▶ Ledian

EVOLUTION

LEDYBA
Five Star Pokémon

Ledyba are easily frightened when alone, but in groups, they are active and rambunctious. They communicate with other Ledyba using scent. This Bug-and-Flying-type doesn't like winter; when it gets cold, Ledyba from all over will come together and huddle up to keep warm.

HOW TO SAY IT: LEH-dee-bah
TYPE: Bug-Flying
ABILITY: Swarm/Early Bird
HEIGHT: 3' 03"
WEIGHT: 23.8 lbs.
POSSIBLE MOVES: Tackle, Supersonic, Comet Punch, Light Screen, Reflect, Safeguard, Mach Punch, Baton Pass, Silver Wind, Agility, Swift, Double-Edge, Bug Buzz

Ledyba   Ledian

EVOLUTION

LUGIA
LEGENDARY POKÉMON
Diving Pokémon

Lugia is known as the guardian of the seas. Its powers are so strong that it prefers to spend its time at the bottom of the ocean, where it sleeps in a deep-sea trench. According to ancient myth, if Lugia flaps its wings, it causes a forty-day storm.

HOW TO SAY IT: LOO-gee-uh
TYPE: Psychic-Flying
ABILITY: Pressure
HEIGHT: 17' 01"
WEIGHT: 476.2 lbs.
POSSIBLE MOVES: Whirlwind, Weather Ball, Gust, Dragon Rush, Extrasensory, Rain Dance, Hydro Pump, Aeroblast, Punishment, AncientPower, Safeguard, Recover, Future Sight, Natural Gift, Calm Mind, Sky Attack

DOES NOT EVOLVE

MAGBY

Live Coal Pokémon

HOW TO SAY IT: MAG-bee
TYPE: Fire
ABILITY: Flame Body
HEIGHT: 2' 04"
WEIGHT: 47.2 lbs.
POSSIBLE MOVES: Smog, Leer, Ember, SmokeScreen, Faint Attack, Fire Spin, Confuse Ray, Fire Punch, Lava Plume, Flamethrower, Sunny Day, Fire Blast

Magby is found primarily in volcanic craters. Its body temperature is about 1,100 degrees Fahrenheit. That's one hot Pokémon! As Magby breathes in and out, red hot coals drip from its nose and mouth. You can tell whether a Magby is healthy or not by its flames — if they are yellow, it's in good health.

Magby   Magmar   Magmortar   EVOLUTION

MAGCARGO
Lava Pokémon

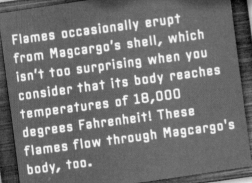

Flames occasionally erupt from Magcargo's shell, which isn't too surprising when you consider that its body reaches temperatures of 18,000 degrees Fahrenheit! These flames flow through Magcargo's body, too.

HOW TO SAY IT: mag-CAR-go
TYPE: Fire-Rock
ABILITY: Magma Armor/ Flame Body
HEIGHT: 2' 07"
WEIGHT: 121.3 lbs.
POSSIBLE MOVES: Yawn, Smog, Ember, Rock Throw, Harden, Recover, AncientPower, Amnesia, Lava Plume, Rock Slide, Body Slam, Flamethrower, Earth Power

Slugma ....> Magcargo

EVOLUTION

MANTINE
Kite Pokémon

Mantine like to swim in packs when the water is calm. If they build up enough speed, they may shoot out of the water and seem to fly across the waves. Mantine never seems to mind the tiny Remoraid that attach themselves to it, scavenging for leftovers.

HOW TO SAY IT: MAN-tine
TYPE: Water-Flying
ABILITY: Swift Swim/ Water Absorb
HEIGHT: 6' 11"
WEIGHT: 485 lbs.
POSSIBLE MOVES: Psybeam, Bullet Seed, Signal Beam, Tackle, Bubble, Supersonic, BubbleBeam, Headbutt, Agility, Wing Attack, Water Pulse, Take Down, Confuse Ray, Bounce, Aqua Ring, Hydro Pump

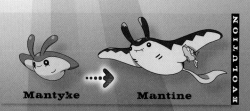

Mantyke ..... > Mantine

EVOLUTION

MAREEP
Wool Pokémon

Mareep may look soft and cuddly, but its fleece packs a powerful electrical charge. The fleece can double in size as Mareep stores up more static electicity. Touching Mareep can be a shocking experience! It sheds its fleece in the summer, but it only takes a week to grow it back in full.

HOW TO SAY IT: mah-REEP
TYPE: Electric
ABILITY: Static
HEIGHT: 2' 00"
WEIGHT: 17.2 lbs.
POSSIBLE MOVES: Tackle, Growl, ThunderShock, Thunder Wave, Cotton Spore, Charge, Discharge, Signal Beam, Light Screen, Power Gem, Thunder

Mareep   Flaaffy   Ampharos   EVOLUTION

MARILL
Aqua Mouse Pokémon

The ball on the end of Marill's tail isn't filled with air, but with special oil that's lighter than water. It uses its tail as a float so it can dive underwater, where it eats the plants that grow on river bottoms. Marill's tail keeps it afloat even when the water current becomes vicious.

HOW TO SAY IT: MARE-rull
TYPE: Water
ABILITY: Thick Fat/ Huge Power
HEIGHT: 1' 04"
WEIGHT: 18.7 lbs.
POSSIBLE MOVES: Tackle, Defense Curl, Tail Whip, Water Gun, Rollout, BubbleBeam, Aqua Ring, Double-Edge, Rain Dance, Aqua Tail, Hydro Pump

Azurill ....➤ Marill ....➤ Azumarill

EVOLUTION

MEGANIUM

Herb Pokémon

The aroma that wafts from around Meganium's neck has the power to calm and soothe angry feelings. Its breath is powerful, too — it can bring dead plants and flowers back to life.

HOW TO SAY IT:
meg-GAY-nee-um
TYPE: Grass
ABILITY: Overgrow
HEIGHT: 5' 11"
WEIGHT: 221.6 lbs.
POSSIBLE MOVES: Tackle, Growl, Razor Leaf, PoisonPowder, Synthesis, Reflect, Magical Leaf, Natural Gift, Petal Dance, Sweet Scent, Light Screen, Body Slam, Safeguard, Aromatherapy, SolarBeam

Chikorita   Bayleef   Meganium

EVOLUTION

MILTANK

Milk Cow Pokémon

Miltank's milk is highly nutritious, making it the perfect drink for those who are ill and exhausted. Children who drink Miltank's milk are said to grow up to become strong and healthy.

HOW TO SAY IT: MIL-tank
TYPE: Normal
ABILITY: Thick Fat/Scrappy
HEIGHT: 3' 11"
WEIGHT: 166.4 lbs.
POSSIBLE MOVES: Tackle, Growl, Defense Curl, Stomp, Milk Drink, Bide, Rollout, Body Slam, Zen Headbutt, Captivate, Gyro Ball, Heal Bell, Wake-Up Slap

DOES NOT EVOLVE

MISDREAVUS

Screech Pokémon

HOW TO SAY IT:
miss-DREE-vus
TYPE: Ghost
ABILITY: Levitate
HEIGHT: 2' 04"
WEIGHT: 2.2 lbs.
POSSIBLE MOVES: Growl, Psywave, Spite, Astonish, Confuse Ray, Mean Look, Psybeam, Pain Split, Payback, Shadow Ball, Perish Song, Grudge, Power Gem

This ghostly Pokémon likes to sneak up on people and pull their hair, mostly for the fun of catching the shocked expressions on their terrified faces! It also likes to howl and shriek to startle innocent people at night. It feeds on the fear that its banshee-like shriek creates.

Misdreavus ➡ Mismagius

EVOLUTION

MURKROW
Darkness Pokémon

Some believe that if Murkrow is being pursued, it will lead its assailant into the mountains, where the attacker will be lost forever! Many people fear this Pokémon. Spotting it at night is said to be very bad luck.

HOW TO SAY IT: MUR-crow
TYPE: Dark-Flying
ABILITY: Insomnia/ Super Luck
HEIGHT: 1' 08"
WEIGHT: 4.6 lbs.
POSSIBLE MOVES: Peck, Astonish, Pursuit, Haze, Wing Attack, Night Shade, Assurance, Taunt, Faint Attack, Mean Look, Sucker Punch

Murkrow ····▶ Honchkrow   EVOLUTION

NATU
Tiny Bird Pokémon

Natu is a Psychic-and-Flying-type, but its wings are not yet fully grown, so it can't fly — it must skip around on the ground to find food. Occasionally, it hops high enough to reach a tree branch. Natu is so agile it can pick food from cacti without getting pricked.

HOW TO SAY IT: NAH-too
TYPE: Psychic-Flying
ABILITY: Synchronize/Early Bird
HEIGHT: 0' 08"
WEIGHT: 4.4 lbs.
POSSIBLE MOVES: Peck, Leer, Night Shade, Teleport, Lucky Chant, Miracle Eye, Me First, Confuse Ray, Wish, Psycho Shift, Future Sight, Ominous Wind, Power Swap, Guard Swap, Psychic

Natu   Xatu

EVOLUTION

NOCTOWL
Owl Pokémon

Noctowl's eyes are special — they focus even the tiniest shred of light and use it to see things in the dark. These eyes allow Noctowl to hunt effectively at night. When Noctowl is thinking, it turns its head sharply. This seems to help it concentrate its brain power.

HOW TO SAY IT: NAHK-towl
TYPE: Normal-Flying
ABILITY: Insomnia/ Keen Eye
HEIGHT: 5' 03"
WEIGHT: 89.9 lbs.
POSSIBLE MOVES: Sky Attack, Tackle, Growl, Foresight, Hypnosis, Peck, Uproar, Reflect, Confusion, Take Down, Air Slash, Zen Headbutt, Extrasensory, Psycho Shift, Roost, Dream Eater

Hoothoot ····▶ Noctowl

EVOLUTION

51

OCTILLERY

Jet Pokémon

Octillery lives deep underwater. It prefers rocky holes and rifts on the ocean's bottom. When Octillery runs into trouble, it grabs its foes with its tentacles, and then uses its head to shatter its prey.

HOW TO SAY IT: ock-TILL-er-ree
TYPE: Water
ABILITY: Suction Cups/Sniper
HEIGHT: 2' 11"
WEIGHT: 62.8 lbs.
POSSIBLE MOVES: Gunk Shot, Rock Blast, Water Gun, Constrict, Psybeam, Aurora Beam, BubbleBeam, Focus Energy, Octazooka, Bullet Seed, Wring Out, Signal Beam, Ice Beam, Hyper Beam

Remoraid   Octillery   EVOLUTION

PHANPY
Long Nose Pokémon

Despite its small stature, Phanpy is very powerful. It can even carry a Trainer on its back. Phanpy can nudge people affectionately with its snout, but it's so strong it's been known to send them hurtling through the air!

HOW TO SAY IT: FAN-pee
TYPE: Ground
ABILITY: Pickup
HEIGHT: 1' 08"
WEIGHT: 73.9 lbs.
POSSIBLE MOVES: Odor Sleuth, Tackle, Growl, Defense Curl, Flail, Take Down, Rollout, Natural Gift, Slam, Endure, Charm, Last Resort, Double-Edge

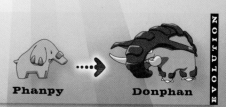

Phanpy ....➡ Donphan

EVOLUTION

PICHU
Tiny Mouse Pokémon

Pichu is one of the smaller Pokémon, but it can pack a powerful electric punch! Pichu sometimes have trouble storing electricity, so they often send out stray jolts when surprised. They also like to play with one another by touching tails and discharging power.

HOW TO SAY IT: PEE-choo
TYPE: Electric
ABILITY: Static
HEIGHT: 1' 00"
WEIGHT: 4.4 lbs.
POSSIBLE MOVES:
ThunderShock, Charm, Tail Whip, Thunder Wave, Sweet Kiss, Nasty Plot

Pichu ····▶ Pikachu ····▶ Raichu

EVOLUTION

PILOSWINE
Swine Pokémon

HOW TO SAY IT: PILE-oh-swine

TYPE: Ice-Ground

ABILITY: Oblivious/Snow Cloak

HEIGHT: 3' 07"

WEIGHT: 123.0 lbs.

POSSIBLE MOVES:

AncientPower, Peck, Odor Sleuth, Mud Sport, Powder Snow, Mud-Slap, Endure, Mud Bomb, Icy Wind, Ice Fang, Take Down, Fury Attack, Earthquake, Mist, Blizzard, Amnesia

Piloswine is so hairy that it has a hard time seeing. So it uses its nose to sniff out its habitat. Since it can't see well, Piloswine will charge an attacker repeatedly.

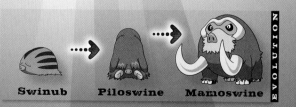

Swinub   Piloswine   Mamoswine   EVOLUTION

PINECO
Bagworm Pokémon

Pineco hardly ever moves, but it can still protect itself by adding layers of tree bark to its shell. This shell protects it from Flying-type Pokémon, who might peck it by accident, thinking it's a pine cone.

HOW TO SAY IT: PINE-co
TYPE: Bug
ABILITY: Sturdy
HEIGHT: 2' 00"
WEIGHT: 15.9 lbs.
POSSIBLE MOVES: Tackle, Protect, Selfdestruct, Bug Bite, Take Down, Rapid Spin, Bide, Natural Gift, Spikes, Payback, Explosion, Iron Defense, Gyro Ball, Double-Edge

Pineco   Forretress   EVOLUTION

POLITOED
Frog Pokémon

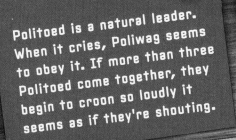

Politoed is a natural leader. When it cries, Poliwag seems to obey it. If more than three Politoed come together, they begin to croon so loudly it seems as if they're shouting.

HOW TO SAY IT: POL-ee-toad
TYPE: Water
ABILITY: Water Absorb/Damp
HEIGHT: 3' 07"
WEIGHT: 74.7 lbs.
POSSIBLE MOVES: BubbleBeam, Hypnosis, DoubleSlap, Perish Song, Swagger, Bounce, Hyper Voice

Poliwag ·····➤ Poliwhirl ·····➤ Politoed

EVOLUTION

PORYGON2
Virtual Pokémon

Porygon2 is the Evolution of Porygon, the first artificially created Pokémon. Despite the fact that it's computerized, it occasionally performs moves that were not programmed. Porygon2 cannot fly, but it was originally intended for space exploration.

HOW TO SAY IT:
POR-ree-gon-too
TYPE: Normal
ABILITY: Trace/Download
HEIGHT: 2' 00"
WEIGHT: 71.6 lbs.
POSSIBLE MOVES: Conversion 2, Tackle, Conversion, Defense Curl, Psybeam, Agility, Recover, Magnet Rise, Signal Beam, Recycle, Discharge, Lock-On, Tri Attack, Magic Coat, Zap Cannon, Hyper Beam

Porygon　Porygon2　Porygon-Z

EVOLUTION

PUPITAR

Hard Shell Pokémon

HOW TO SAY IT: PUE-puh-tar
TYPE: Rock-Ground
ABILITY: Shed Skin
HEIGHT: 3' 11"
WEIGHT: 335.1 lbs.
POSSIBLE MOVES: Bite, Leer, Sandstorm, Screech, Rock Slide, Scary Face, Thrash, Dark Pulse, Payback, Crunch, Earthquake, Stone Edge, Hyper Beam

Pupitar may be stuck in a rock-hard casing, but it is still able to move about at will. When it builds up gases in its body, Pupitar can shoot itself up like a rocket. It is hard, fast, and strong.

Larvitar ....➤ Pupitar ....➤ Tyranitar

EVOLUTION

QUAGSIRE
Water Fish Pokémon

Quagsire is so easygoing it often bumps its head on boulders and boats as it swims. These bumps don't seem to bother Quagsire one bit. It's so relaxed, it waits at the bottom of rivers, just hoping food will wander into its belly.

HOW TO SAY IT: KWAG-sire
TYPE: Water-Ground
ABILITY: Damp/Water Absorb
HEIGHT: 4' 07"
WEIGHT: 165.3 lbs.
POSSIBLE MOVES: Water Gun, Tail Whip, Mud Sport, Mud Shot, Slam, Mud Bomb, Amnesia, Yawn, Earthquake, Rain Dance, Mist, Haze, Muddy Water

Wooper ....➤ Quagsire

EVOLUTION

QUILAVA
Volcano Pokémon

HOW TO SAY IT: kwi-LA-va
TYPE: Fire
ABILITY: Blaze
HEIGHT: 2' 11"
WEIGHT: 41.9 lbs.
POSSIBLE MOVES: Tackle, Leer, SmokeScreen, Ember, Quick Attack, Flame Wheel, Defense Curl, Swift, Lava Plume, Flamethrower, Rollout, Double-Edge, Eruption

Quilava is completely covered with fireproof fur. It can endure any and every kind of flame. If you find yourself facing this Fire-type's backside, watch out — that usually means Quilava is about to launch a massive flame attack! When it's ready to fight, the flames around it will burn even more intently, intimidating its foes.

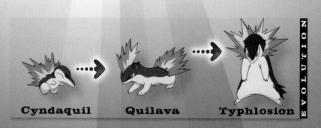

Cyndaquil   Quilava   Typhlosion

EVOLUTION

QWILFISH
Balloon Pokémon

Qwilfish inject a toxin that will cause its victim to faint instantly. In order to fire this toxin, Qwilfish must drink over two gallons of water in one gulp! Despite the danger it poses to others in the water, Qwilfish is not a very good swimmer.

HOW TO SAY IT: KWIL-fish
TYPE: Water-Poison
ABILITY: Poison Point/ Swift Swim
HEIGHT: 1' 08"
WEIGHT: 8.6 lbs.
POSSIBLE MOVES: Spikes, Tackle, Poison Sting, Harden, Minimize, Water Gun, Rollout, Toxic Spikes, Stockpile, Spit Up, Revenge, Brine, Pin Missile, Take Down, Aqua Tail, Poison Jab, Destiny Bond, Hydro Pump

DOES NOT EVOLVE

RAIKOU
LEGENDARY POKÉMON
Thunder Pokémon

Raikou's piercing cry sounds like the crashing of thunder. The rain cloud it carries on its back fires massive thunderbolts. According to legend, this mysterious Pokémon descended to the world with lightning.

HOW TO SAY IT: RYE-coo
TYPE: Electric
ABILITY: Pressure
HEIGHT: 6' 03"
WEIGHT: 392.4 lbs.
POSSIBLE MOVES: Bite, Leer, ThunderShock, Roar, Quick Attack, Spark, Reflect, Crunch, Thunder Fang, Discharge, Extrasensory, Rain Dance, Calm Mind, Thunder

DOES NOT EVOLVE

REMORAID

Jet Pokémon

Remoraid use their dorsal fins as suction cups to cling to the undersides of Mantine. This way, Remoraid can scavenge for Mantine's leftover food. But Remoraid isn't totally dependent on Mantine. With the powerful squirts of water it shoots out of its mouth, it can strike moving prey from three hundred feet away.

HOW TO SAY IT: REM-oh-raid
TYPE: Water
ABILITY: Hustle/Sniper
HEIGHT: 2' 00"
WEIGHT: 26.5 lbs.
POSSIBLE MOVES: Water Gun, Lock-On, Psybeam, Aurora Beam, BubbleBeam, Focus Energy, Bullet Seed, Water Pulse, Signal Beam, Ice Beam, Hyper Beam

Remoraid ·····➤ Octillery

EVOLUTION

SCIZOR

Pincer Pokémon

HOW TO SAY IT: SI-zor
TYPE: Bug-Steel
ABILITY: Swarm/Technician
HEIGHT: 5' 11"
WEIGHT: 260.1 lbs.
POSSIBLE MOVES: Bullet Punch, Quick Attack, Leer, Focus Energy, Pursuit, False Swipe, Agility, Metal Claw, Fury Cutter, Slash, Razor Wind, Iron Defense, X-Scissor, Night Slash, Double Hit, Iron Head, Swords Dance, Feint

In battle, Scizor brandishes its pincers into the air, making it appear to have three heads. This move has been known to intimidate opponents. When Scizor beats its wings rapidly, it can regulate its body temperature.

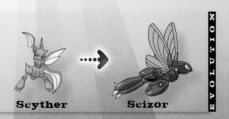

Scyther ·····➤ Scizor

EVOLUTION

SENTRET

Scout Pokémon

HOW TO SAY IT: SEN-tret
TYPE: Normal
ABILITY: Run Away/Keen Eye
HEIGHT: 2' 07"
WEIGHT: 13.2 lbs.
POSSIBLE MOVES: Scratch, Foresight, Defense Curl, Quick Attack, Fury Swipes, Helping Hand, Follow Me, Slam, Rest, Sucker Punch, Amnesia, Baton Pass, Me First, Hyper Voice

Sentret is very cautious and wary of danger. It can stand straight up on its tail to survey its surroundings. If it spots any oncoming danger, it will cry out to alert the rest of its kind.

Sentret ·····▶ **Furret**

EVOLUTION

SHUCKLE

Mold Pokémon

HOW TO SAY IT: SHUCK-kull
TYPE: Bug-Rock
ABILITY: Sturdy Gluttony
HEIGHT: 2' 00"
WEIGHT: 45.2 lbs.
POSSIBLE MOVES: Withdraw, Constrict, Bide, Encore, Safeguard, Wrap, Rest, Gastro Acid, Bug Bite, Power Trick

Shuckle conceals itself beneath rocks and lies there, still, in order to avoid being detected by foes. It has an odd habit of storing berries in its shell. Over time, the berries turn into a delicious juice.

SKARMORY
Armor Bird Pokémon

Skarmory is clad in iron-hard armor. Despite its heaviness, it is fast! Skarmory flies at speeds of one hundred and eighty miles per hour.

HOW TO SAY IT: SKAR-more-ree
TYPE: Steel-Flying
ABILITY: Keen Eye/Sturdy
HEIGHT: 5' 07"
WEIGHT: 111.3 lbs.
POSSIBLE MOVES: Leer, Peck, Sand-Attack, Swift, Agility, Fury Attack, Feint, Air Cutter, Spikes, Metal Sound, Steel Wing, Air Slash, Slash, Night Slash

DOES NOT EVOLVE

SKIPLOOM
Cottonweed Pokémon

HOW TO SAY IT: SKIP-loom
TYPE: Grass-Flying
ABILITY: Chlorophyll/Leaf Guard
HEIGHT: 2' 00"
WEIGHT: 2.2 lbs.
POSSIBLE MOVES: Splash, Synthesis, Tail Whip, Tackle, PoisonPowder, Stun Spore, Sleep Powder, Bullet Seed, Leech Seed, Mega Drain, Cotton Spore, U-turn, Worry Seed, Giga Drain, Bounce, Memento

When daylight comes, Skiploom opens its petals to drink in the sunshine. It can even float through the air to get closer to the sun. The large blossom on its head opens and closes as the temperature increases and decreases.

Hoppip   Skiploom   Jumpluff

SLOWKING
Royal Pokémon

HOW TO SAY IT: SLOW-king
TYPE: Water-Psychic
ABILITY: Oblivious/Own Tempo
HEIGHT: 6' 07"
WEIGHT: 175.3 lbs.
POSSIBLE MOVES: Power Gem, Hidden Power, Curse, Yawn, Tackle, Growl, Water Gun, Confusion, Disable, Headbutt, Water Pulse, Zen Headbutt, Nasty Plot, Swagger, Psychic, Trump Card, Psych Up

Slowking is a very unusual Pokémon. When the Shellder on its head bit down, toxins unleashed amazing skills in Slowking. This Water-and-Psychic-type is unusually intelligent. It's also able to keep cool under pressure.

Slowpoke   Slowking

EVOLUTION

SLUGMA

Lava Pokémon

HOW TO SAY IT: SLUG-ma
TYPE: Fire
ABILITY: Magma Armor/
Flame Body
HEIGHT: 2' 04"
WEIGHT: 77.2 lbs.
POSSIBLE MOVES: Yawn,
Smog, Ember, Rock
Throw, Harden, Recover,
AncientPower, Amnesia,
Lava Plume, Rock Slide,
Body Slam, Flamethrower,
Earth Power

Slugma live in volcanic areas. Magma is the main element of their makeup. If they don't move continually, they'll harden. So they slither around looking for warm spots. They move so constantly, they don't even stop for sleep!

Slugma ····▶ Magcargo

EVOLUTION

SMEARGLE
Painter Pokémon

Smeargle's tail is unique. It exudes liquid that Smeargle uses as paint to show its turf. Smeargle can make over five thousand different marks.

HOW TO SAY IT: SMEAR-gull
TYPE: Normal
ABILITY: Own Tempo/ Technician
HEIGHT: 3' 11"
WEIGHT: 127.9 lbs.
POSSIBLE MOVES: Sketch

DOES NOT EVOLVE

SMOOCHUM

Kiss Pokémon

Smoochum tilts its head back and forth as if it's trying to kiss someone. Since its lips are the most responsive part of its body, it uses them to check things out. Smoochum's lips have the power to remember all the good things it likes — and the bad things it dislikes.

HOW TO SAY IT: SMOO-chum
TYPE: Ice-Psychic
ABILITY: Oblivious/Forewarn
HEIGHT: 1' 04"
WEIGHT: 13.2 lbs.
POSSIBLE MOVES: Pound, Lick, Sweet Kiss, Powder Snow, Confusion, Sing, Mean Look, Fake Tears, Lucky Chant, Avalanche, Psychic, Copycat, Perish Song, Blizzard

Smoochum ····> Jynx

EVOLUTION

SNEASEL
Sharp Claw Pokémon

Sneasel plunders eggs from nests, then eats them. Its paws hide sharp claws, which it uses to startle its enemies and tear at its prey. In battle, Sneasel will stop at nothing — not while its opponent is still moving.

HOW TO SAY IT: SNEE-zul
TYPE: Dark-Ice
ABILITY: Inner Focus/ Keen Eye
HEIGHT: 2' 11"
WEIGHT: 61.7 lbs.
POSSIBLE MOVES: Scratch, Leer, Taunt, Quick Attack, Screech, Faint Attack, Fury Swipes, Agility, Icy Wind, Slash, Beat Up, Metal Claw, Ice Shard

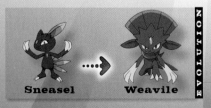

Sneasel ....▶ Weavile

EVOLUTION

SNUBBULL
Fairy Pokémon

Snubbull looks grouchy, but it's actually very sweet and affectionate. Some women find it adorable. Nonetheless, small creatures tend to be terrified by its fierce expression.

HOW TO SAY IT: SNUB-bull
TYPE: Normal
ABILITY: Intimidate/ Run Away
HEIGHT: 2' 00"
WEIGHT: 17.2 lbs.
POSSIBLE MOVES: Ice Fang, Fire Fang, Thunder Fang, Tackle, Scary Face, Tail Whip, Charm, Bite, Lick, Headbutt, Roar, Rage, Take Down, Payback, Crunch

Snubbull   Granbull

EVOLUTION

SPINARAK
String Spit Pokémon

Spinarak are famous for their patience. After they spin their light but sturdy webs, they will sit in the same position for days until they catch their prey.

HOW TO SAY IT:
SPIN-uh-rack

TYPE: Bug-Poison

ABILITY: Swarm/Insomnia

HEIGHT: 1' 08"

WEIGHT: 18.7 lbs.

POSSIBLE MOVES: Poison Sting, String Shot, Scary Face, Constrict, Leech Life, Night Shade, Shadow Sneak, Fury Swipes, Sucker Punch, Spider Web, Agility, Pin Missile, Psychic, Poison Jab

Spinarak   Ariados   EVOLUTION

STANTLER

Big Horn Pokémon

If you stare too long at Stantler's antlers, you will lose control of your senses and fall down. Stantler's antlers somehow alter the air around them, causing the real world to seem warped.

HOW TO SAY IT: STAN-tler
TYPE: Normal
ABILITY: Intimidate/Frisk
HEIGHT: 4' 07"
WEIGHT: 157.0 lbs.
POSSIBLE MOVES: Tackle, Leer, Astonish, Hypnosis, Stomp, Sand-Attack, Take Down, Confuse Ray, Calm Mind, Role Play, Zen Headbutt, Imprison, Captivate, Me First

DOES NOT EVOLVE

STEELIX

Iron Snake Pokémon

Steelix lives deep underground, where the earth's pressure has made its body harder than diamonds. Steelix can see in the dark and chew through boulders.

HOW TO SAY IT: STEE-licks
TYPE: Steel-Ground
ABILITY: Rock Head/Sturdy
HEIGHT: 30' 02"
WEIGHT: 881.8 lbs.
POSSIBLE MOVES: Thunder Fang, Ice Fang, Fire Fang, Mud Sport, Tackle, Harden, Bind, Screech, Rock Throw, Rage, Rock Tomb, Sandstorm, Slam, Rock Polish, DragonBreath, Curse, Iron Tail, Crunch, Double-Edge, Stone Edge

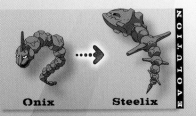

Onix   Steelix

EVOLUTION

SUDOWOODO

Imitation Pokémon

HOW TO SAY IT:
SOO-doe-WOO-doe
TYPE: Rock
ABILITY: Sturdy/Rock Head
HEIGHT: 3' 11"
WEIGHT: 83.8 lbs.
POSSIBLE MOVES: Wood Hammer, Copycat, Flail, Low Kick, Rock Throw, Mimic, Block, Faint Attack, Rock Tomb, Rock Slide, Slam, Sucker Punch, Double-Edge, Hammer Arm

Sudowoodo appear to be made of wood, but they're more like rock. They use their appearance to hide and avoid detection when they're under attack. They hate water and will disappear if it begins to rain.

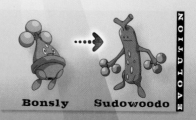

Bonsly   Sudowoodo   EVOLUTION

SUICUNE
LEGENDARY POKÉMON
Aurora Pokémon

According to legend, Suicune is the embodiment of the north wind. It has the power to purify polluted waters.

HOW TO SAY IT: SWEE-koon
TYPE: Water
ABILITY: Pressure
HEIGHT: 6' 07"
WEIGHT: 412.3 lbs.
POSSIBLE MOVES: Bite, Leer, BubbleBeam, Rain Dance, Gust, Aurora Beam, Mist, Mirror Coat, Ice Fang, Tailwind, Extrasensory, Hydro Pump, Calm Mind, Blizzard

DOES NOT EVOLVE

SUNFLORA
Sun Pokémon

HOW TO SAY IT: SUN-FLOR-a
TYPE: Grass
ABILITY: Chlorophyll/Solar Power
HEIGHT: 2' 07"
WEIGHT: 18.7 lbs.
POSSIBLE MOVES: Absorb, Pound, Growth, Mega Drain, Ingrain, GrassWhistle, Leech Seed, Bullet Seed, Worry Seed, Razor Leaf, Petal Dance, Sunny Day, SolarBeam, Leaf Storm

During the day, Sunflora rush around converting the sun's rays into energy. They will travel constantly to find sunshine. At night, Sunflora comes to a complete stop, closes its petals, and becomes perfectly still until sunrise.

Sunkern   Sunflora

EVOLUTION

SUNKERN
Seed Pokémon

HOW TO SAY IT: SUN-kern
TYPE: Grass
ABILITY: Chlorophyll/Solar Power
HEIGHT: 1' 00"
WEIGHT: 4.0 lbs.
POSSIBLE MOVES: Absorb, Growth, Mega Drain, Ingrain, GrassWhistle, Leech Seed, Endeavor, Worry Seed, Razor Leaf, Synthesis, Sunny Day, Giga Drain, Seed Bomb

Sunkern drops out of the sky unexpectedly in the morning. It lives solely by drinking the dewdrops that accumulate under the leaves of plants. If it's attacked, it will shake its leaves violently.

Sunkern   Sunflora

EVOLUTION

SWINUB

Pig Pokémon

If Swinub smells something good, it dashes off to find the source of the aroma. It will root around in the ground to dig up the food, which often turns out to be mushrooms. Sometimes Swinub finds hot springs this way.

HOW TO SAY IT: SWY-nub
TYPE: Ice-Ground
ABILITY: Oblivious/ Snow Cloak
HEIGHT: 1' 04"
WEIGHT: 14.3 lbs.
POSSIBLE MOVES: Tackle, Odor Sleuth, Mud Sport, Powder Snow, Mud-Slap, Endure, Mud Bomb, Icy Wind, Ice Shard, Take Down, Earthquake, Mist, Blizzard, Amnesia

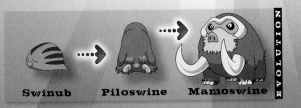

Swinub → Piloswine → Mamoswine

EVOLUTION

TEDDIURSA
Little Bear Pokémon

When Teddiursa finds honey, the crescent mark on its head glows. It likes to lick its paws because they are always soaked with honey. Teddiursa is very resourceful — it starts hoarding food in many different hiding places long before winter begins.

HOW TO SAY IT: TED-dy-UR-sa
TYPE: Normal
ABILITY: Pickup/ Quick Feet
HEIGHT: 2' 00"
WEIGHT: 19.4 lbs.
POSSIBLE MOVES: Covet, Scratch, Leer, Lick, Fake Tears, Fury Swipes, Faint Attack, Sweet Scent, Slash, Charm, Rest, Snore, Thrash, Fling

Teddiursa   Ursaring

EVOLUTION

TOGEPI
Spike Ball Pokémon

HOW TO SAY IT: TOE-geh-pee
TYPE: Normal
ABILITY: Hustle/Serene Grace
HEIGHT: 1' 00"
WEIGHT: 3.3 lbs.
POSSIBLE MOVES: Growl, Charm, Metronome, Sweet Kiss, Yawn, Encore, Follow Me, Wish, AncientPower, Safeguard, Baton Pass, Double-Edge, Last Resort

According to legend, anyone who can make a sleeping Togepi stand up will find happiness. This little Pokémon's shell is filled with joy, and it will share its good luck with those who treat it kindly.

Togepi → Togetic → Togekiss

EVOLUTION

TOGETIC
Happiness Pokémon

HOW TO SAY IT: TOE-geh-tick
TYPE: Normal-Flying
ABILITY: Hustle/
Serene Grace
HEIGHT: 2' 00"
WEIGHT: 7.1 lbs.
POSSIBLE MOVES: Magical Leaf, Growl, Charm, Metronome, Sweet Kiss, Yawn, Encore, Follow Me, Wish, AncientPower, Safeguard, Baton Pass, Double-Edge, Last Resort

Togetic is a mysterious Pokémon. Some believe that it will reveal itself to kindhearted people and shower them with a glowing powder called "joy dust." This Pokémon is somehow able to hover in the air without flapping its wings.

Togepi   Togetic   Togekiss

EVOLUTION

TOTODILE
Big Jaw Pokémon

This little Water-type is one of the three Pokémon available to new Trainers in Johto. Totodile is a great battler, with super-strong jaws that can crush just about everything. In fact, Totodile will take a bite of almost anything that moves — even its own Trainer. So be careful!

HOW TO SAY IT: TOE-toe-dyle
TYPE: Water
ABILITY: Torrent
HEIGHT: 2' 00"
WEIGHT: 20.9 lbs.
POSSIBLE MOVES: Scratch, Leer, Water Gun, Rage, Bite, Scary Face, Ice Fang, Flail, Crunch, Slash, Screech, Thrash, Aqua Tail, Superpower, Hydro Pump

Totodile ···▶ Croconaw ···▶ Feraligatr

EVOLUTION

TYPHLOSION
Volcano Pokémon

HOW TO SAY IT: tie-FLOW-zhun
TYPE: Fire
ABILITY: Blaze
HEIGHT: 5' 07"
WEIGHT: 175.3 lbs.
POSSIBLE MOVES: Gyro Ball, Tackle, Leer, SmokeScreen, Ember, Quick Attack, Flame Wheel, Defense Curl, Swift, Lava Plume, Flamethrower, Rollout, Double-Edge, Eruption

Typhlosion has a powerful technique: It rubs its fiery fur together to cause enormous explosions. In battle, it creates walls of shimmering heat to hide behind, and then blasts foes with intense fiery attacks. When this powerful Fire-type is mad, its fur gets so hot that anything it touches will immediately catch fire.

Cyndaquil   Quilava   Typhlosion   EVOLUTION

TYRANITAR
Armor Pokémon

Tyranitar is so strong it can change the landscape around it! If it gets angry, it will take down mountains and bury rivers. Tyranitar has an insolent nature. It is nearly impervious to attack, so it is very eager to challenge foes.

HOW TO SAY IT:
tie-RAN-uh-tar
TYPE: Rock-Dark
ABILITY: Sand Stream
HEIGHT: 6' 07"
WEIGHT: 445.3 lbs.
POSSIBLE MOVES: Thunder Fang, Ice Fang, Fire Fang, Bite, Leer, Sandstorm, Screech, Rock Slide, Scary Face, Thrash, Dark Pulse, Payback, Crunch, Earthquake, Stone Edge, Hyper Beam

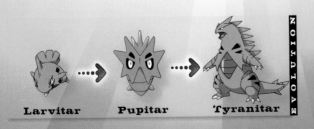

Larvitar ·····> Pupitar ·····> Tyranitar

EVOLUTION

TYROGUE
Scuffle Pokémon

Tyrogue is small, but tough! It is very hotheaded and has a very short temper. It will attack anyone and anything at will. Tyrogue is overflowing with energy and will continue fighting even if it's losing, just so it can keep on building up strength.

HOW TO SAY IT: tie-ROAG
TYPE: Fighting
ABILITY: Guts/Steadfast
HEIGHT: 2' 04"
WEIGHT: 46.3 lbs.
POSSIBLE MOVES: Tackle, Helping Hand, Fake Out, Foresight

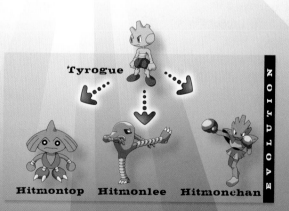

Tyrogue

Hitmontop   Hitmonlee   Hitmonchan

EVOLUTION

UMBREON

Moonlight Pokémon

HOW TO SAY IT: UMM-bree-on
TYPE: Dark
ABILITY: Synchronize
HEIGHT: 3' 03"
WEIGHT: 59.5 lbs.
POSSIBLE MOVES: Tail Whip, Tackle, Helping Hand, Sand-Attack, Pursuit, Quick Attack, Confuse Ray, Faint Attack, Assurance, Last Resort, Mean Look, Screech, Moonlight, Guard Swap

Umbreon evolved when moonlight changed Eevee's genetic structure. When night falls, the rings on Umbreon's body begin to glow, casting fear in the hearts of its foes. When attacked, Umbreon can secrete venomous sweat in order to keep itself from harm.

Eevee ....> Umbreon

EVOLUTION

UNOWN

Symbol Pokémon

HOW TO SAY IT: un-KNOWN
TYPE: Psychic
ABILITY: Levitate
HEIGHT: 1' 08"
WEIGHT: 11.0 lbs.
POSSIBLE MOVES:
Hidden Power

You can sometimes see Unown stuck to the walls of caves. Unown use telepathy to communicate. No one knows which came first, Unown or language.

URSARING
Hibernator Pokémon

Ursaring has the amazing ability to detect aromas. It can find any food, even if it's buried underground. Ursaring is good at climbing, but it likes to find food by breaking branches and letting berries fall to the ground.

HOW TO SAY IT: UR-sa-ring
TYPE: Normal
ABILITY: Guts/Quick Feet
HEIGHT: 5' 11"
WEIGHT: 277.3 lbs.
POSSIBLE MOVES: Covet, Scratch, Leer, Lick, Fake Tears, Fury Swipes, Faint Attack, Sweet Scent, Slash, Scary Face, Rest, Snore, Thrash, Hammer Arm

Teddiursa → Ursaring

EVOLUTION

WOBBUFFET

Patient Pokémon

HOW TO SAY IT: WAH-buf-fett
TYPE: Psychic
ABILITY: Shadow Tag
HEIGHT: 4' 03"
WEIGHT: 62.8 lbs.
POSSIBLE MOVES: Counter, Mirror Coat, Safeguard, Destiny Bond

Wobbuffet prefers to keep its pitch-black tail hidden. Some believe this is because its tail hides a secret.

Wynaut ....▶ Wobbuffet

EVOLUTION

WOOPER

Water Fish Pokémon

HOW TO SAY IT: WOOP-pur
TYPE: Water-Ground
ABILITY: Damp/Water Absorb
HEIGHT: 1' 04"
WEIGHT: 18.7 lbs.
POSSIBLE MOVES: Water Gun, Tail Whip, Mud Sport, Mud Shot, Slam, Mud Bomb, Amnesia, Yawn, Earthquake, Rain Dance, Mist, Haze, Muddy Water

Wooper live in cold water, but they will leave the water to search for food when the temperature on land gets cold enough. In order to protect itself, it coats its body with a slimy, poisonous film when it walks around on dry land.

Wooper ....▶ Quagsire

EVOLUTION

XATU
Mystic Pokémon

HOW TO SAY IT: ZAH-too
TYPE: Psychic-Flying
ABILITY: Synchronize/
Early Bird
HEIGHT: 4' 11"
WEIGHT: 33.1 lbs.
POSSIBLE MOVES: Peck, Leer,
Night Shade, Teleport,
Lucky Chant, Miracle Eye,
Me First, Confuse Ray,
Tailwind, Wish, Psycho
Shift, Future Sight,
Ominous Wind, Power Swap,
Guard Swap, Psychic

Xatu has the power to look into both the future and the past. Some believe this is why Xatu stands so still and quiet, watching the sun all day.

Natu ····> Xatu

EVOLUTION

91

YANMA
Clear Wing Pokémon

Yanma's big eyes can look everywhere at once — literally! It can scan 360° without turning its head. Its wings can create vibrations that can break glass.

HOW TO SAY IT: YAN-ma
TYPE: Bug-Flying
ABILITY: Speed Boost/ CompoundEyes
HEIGHT: 3' 11"
WEIGHT: 83.8 lbs.
POSSIBLE MOVES: Tackle, Foresight, Quick Attack, Double Team, SonicBoom, Detect, Supersonic, Uproar, Pursuit, AncientPower, Hypnosis, Wing Attack, Screech, U-turn, Air Slash, Bug Buzz

Yanma   Yanmega

EVOLUTION

ASH & FRIENDS APPENDIX

Ash and his friends have met many Pokémon during their adventures. We'll show you some of those Pokémon here. What ties these Pokémon together? Some of these Pokémon were caught in Johto, and some were not. But all of them are species that are native to the Johto Region!

ASH

Ash Ketchum is on a quest to become the world's greatest Pokémon Master. While he was traveling in Johto, Ash caught and befriended many Pokémon. Ash can be hot-headed, but he really cares about his Pokémon. Below are a few he obtained during his travels.

BAYLEEF

PAGE 11

CYNDAQUIL

PAGE 18

HERACROSS

PAGE 28

TOTODILE

PAGE 84

DONPHAN

PAGE 19

BROCK

Brock is a Trainer who wants to become the world's best Pokémon breeder. He's also known for his skill in caring for Pokémon and in making food that both humans and Pokémon adore. Here are a few of the Pokémon who helped him.

CROBAT

PAGE 16

FORRETRESS

PAGE 24

SUDOWOODO
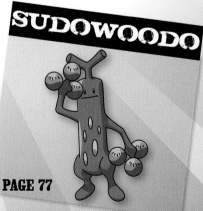

PAGE 77

DAWN

Like Ash, Dawn is on a quest. She wants to become a great Pokémon Coordinator like her mom, Johanna. She carries one of Johanna's ribbons for good luck. Dawn is just starting on her Pokémon journey, but she is always confident. She learns quickly from her mistakes. So far, she has only one Johto Pokémon.

CYNDAQUIL

PAGE 18